Contents

In
1935 if you wanted to
read a good book, you needed
either a lot of money or a library card.
Cheap paperbacks were available, but their
poor production generally mirrored the quality
between the covers. One weekend that year,
Allen Lane, Managing Director of The Bodley Head,
having spent the weekend visiting Agatha Christie,
found himself on a platform at Exeter station trying to
find something to read for his journey back to London.
He was appalled by the quality of the material he had to
choose from. Everything that Allen Lane achieved from that
day until his death in 1970 was based on a passionate belief
in the existence of 'a vast reading public for *intelligent*
books at a low price'. The result of his momentous vision
was the birth not only of Penguin, but of the 'paperback
revolution'. Quality writing became available for the price of
a packet of cigarettes, literature became a mass medium
for the first time, a nation of book-borrowers became a
nation of book-buyers – and the very concept of book
publishing was changed for ever. Those founding
principles – of quality and value, with an overarching
belief in the fundamental importance of reading –
have guided everything the company has
done since 1935. Sir Allen Lane's
pioneering spirit is still very much alive
at Penguin in 2005. Here's to
the next 70 years!

MORE THAN A BUSINESS

'We decided it was time to end the almost customary half-hearted manner in which cheap editions were produced – as though the only people who could possibly want cheap editions must belong to a lower order of intelligence. We, however, believed in the existence in this country of a vast reading public for intelligent books at a low price, and staked everything on it'
Sir Allen Lane, 1902–1970

'The Penguin Books are splendid value for sixpence, so splendid that if other publishers had any sense they would combine against them and suppress them'
George Orwell

'More than a business ... a national cultural asset'
Guardian

'When you look at the whole Penguin achievement you know that it constitutes, in action, one of the more democratic successes of our recent social history'
Richard Hoggart

Murder

JOHN STEINBECK

PENGUIN BOOKS

PENGUIN BOOKS

Published by the Penguin Group
Penguin Books Ltd, 80 Strand, London WC2R ORL, England
Penguin Group (USA) Inc., 375 Hudson Street, New York, New York 10014, USA
Penguin Group (Canada), 10 Alcorn Avenue, Toronto, Ontario, Canada M4V 3B2
(a division of Pearson Penguin Canada Inc.)
Penguin Ireland, 25 St Stephen's Green, Dublin 2, Ireland
(a division of Penguin Books Ltd)
Penguin Group (Australia), 250 Camberwell Road, Camberwell, Victoria 3124,
Australia (a division of Pearson Australia Group Pty Ltd)
Penguin Books India Pvt Ltd, 11 Community Centre,
Panchsheel Park, New Delhi – 110 017, India
Penguin Group (NZ), cnr Airborne and Rosedale Roads, Albany,
Auckland 1310, New Zealand (a division of Pearson New Zealand Ltd)
Penguin Books (South Africa) (Pty) Ltd, 24 Sturdee Avenue,
Rosebank 2196, South Africa

Penguin Books Ltd, Registered Offices: 80 Strand, London WC2R ORL, England

www.penguin.com

The Long Valley first published in the USA by the Viking Press 1938
Published in Penguin Books 1986
This selection published as a Pocket Penguin 2005

1

Set in 11.5/13.5pt Monotype Dante
Typeset by Palimpsest Book Production Limited
Polmont, Stirlingshire
Printed in England by Clays Ltd, St Ives plc

The Chrysanthemums

The high grey-flannel fog of winter closed off the Salinas Valley from the sky and from all the rest of the world. On every side it sat like a lid on the mountains and made of the great valley a closed pot. On the broad, level land floor the gang plows bit deep and left the black earth shining like metal where the shares had cut. On the foothill ranches across the Salinas River, the yellow stubble fields seemed to be bathed in pale cold sunshine, but there was no sunshine in the valley now in December. The thick willow scrub along the river flamed with sharp and positive yellow leaves.

It was a time of quiet and of waiting. The air was cold and tender. A light wind blew up from the southwest so that the farmers were mildly hopeful of a good rain before long; but fog and rain do not go together.

Across the river, on Henry Allen's foothill ranch there was little work to be done, for the hay was cut and stored and the orchards were plowed up to receive the rain deeply when it should come. The cattle on the higher slopes were becoming shaggy and rough-coated.

Elisa Allen, working in her flower garden,

looked down across the yard and saw Henry, her husband, talking to two men in business suits. The three of them stood by the tractor shed, each man with one foot on the side of the little Fordson. They smoked cigarettes and studied the machine as they talked.

Elisa watched them for a moment and then went back to her work. She was thirty-five. Her face was lean and strong and her eyes were as clear as water. Her figure looked blocked and heavy in her gardening costume, a man's black hat pulled low down over her eyes, clodhopper shoes, a figured print dress almost completely covered by a big corduroy apron with four big pockets to hold the snips, the trowel and scratcher, the seeds and the knife she worked with. She wore heavy leather gloves to protect her hands while she worked.

She was cutting down the old year's chrysanthemum stalks with a pair of short and powerful scissors. She looked down toward the men by the tractor shed now and then. Her face was eager and mature and handsome; even her work with the scissors was over-eager, over-powerful. The chrysanthemum stems seemed too small and easy for her energy.

She brushed a cloud of hair out of her eyes with the back of her glove, and left a smudge of earth on her cheek in doing it. Behind her stood the neat white farm house with red geraniums close-banked around it as high as the windows. It was a hard-swept looking little house with hard-polished windows, and a clean mud-mat on the front steps.

Elisa cast another glance toward the tractor shed. The strangers were getting into their Ford coupe. She took off a glove and put her strong fingers down into the forest of new green chrysanthemum sprouts that were growing around the old roots. She spread the leaves and looked down among the close-growing stems. No aphids were there, no sowbugs or snails or cutworms. Her terrier fingers destroyed such pests before they could get started.

Elisa started at the sound of her husband's voice. He had come near quietly, and he leaned over the wire fence that protected her flower garden from cattle and dogs and chickens.

'At it again,' he said. 'You've got a strong new crop coming.'

Elisa straightened her back and pulled on the gardening glove again. 'Yes. They'll be strong this coming year.' In her tone and on her face there was a little smugness.

'You've got a gift with things,' Henry observed. 'Some of those yellow chrysanthemums you had this year were ten inches across. I wish you'd work out in the orchard and raise some apples that big.'

Her eyes sharpened. 'Maybe I could do it, too. I've a gift with things, all right. My mother had it. She could stick anything in the ground and make it grow. She said it was having planters' hands that knew how to do it.'

'Well, it sure works with flowers,' he said.

'Henry, who were those men you were talking to?'

'Why, sure, that's what I came to tell you. They were from the Western Meat Company. I sold those thirty head of three-year-old steers. Got nearly my own price, too.'

'Good,' she said. 'Good for you.'

'And I thought,' he continued, 'I thought how it's Saturday afternoon, and we might go into Salinas for dinner at a restaurant, and then to a picture show – to celebrate, you see.'

'Good,' she repeated. 'Oh, yes. That will be good.'

Henry put on his joking tone. 'There's fights tonight. How'd you like to go to the fights?'

'Oh, no,' she said breathlessly. 'No, I wouldn't like fights.'

'Just fooling, Elisa. We'll go to a movie. Let's see. It's two now. I'm going to take Scotty and bring down those steers from the hill. It'll take us maybe two hours. We'll go in town about five and have dinner at the Cominos Hotel. Like that?'

'Of course I'll like it. It's good to eat away from home.'

'All right, then. I'll go get up a couple of horses.'

She said, 'I'll have plenty of time to transplant some of these sets, I guess.'

She heard her husband calling Scotty down by the barn. And a little later she saw the two men ride up the pale yellow hillside in search of the steers.

There was a little square sandy bed kept for rooting the chrysanthemums. With her trowel she turned the soil over and over, and smoothed it and patted it firm. Then she dug ten parallel trenches to receive the sets. Back at the chrysanthemum bed she pulled out the little crisp shoots, trimmed off the leaves of each one with her scissors and laid it on a small orderly pile.

A squeak of wheels and plod of hoofs came from the road. Elisa looked up. The country road ran along the dense bank of willows and cotton-woods that bordered the river, and up this road came a curious vehicle, curiously drawn. It was an old spring-wagon, with a round canvas top on it like the cover of a prairie schooner. It was drawn by an old bay horse and a little grey-and-white burro. A big stubble-bearded man sat between the cover flaps and drove the crawling team. Underneath the wagon, between the hind wheels, a lean and rangy mongrel dog walked sedately. Words were painted on the canvas, in clumsy, crooked letters. 'Pots, pans, knives, sisors, lawn mores, Fixed.' Two rows of articles, and the triumphantly definitive 'Fixed' below. The black paint had run down in little sharp points beneath each letter.

Elisa, squatting on the ground, watched to see the crazy, loose-jointed wagon pass by. But it didn't pass. It turned into the farm road in front of her house, crooked old wheels skirling and squeaking. The rangy dog darted from between the wheels and ran ahead. Instantly the two ranch shepherds flew out at him. Then all three stopped, and with stiff and quivering tails, with taut straight legs, with ambassadorial dignity, they slowly circled, sniffing daintily. The caravan pulled up to Elisa's wire fence and stopped. Now the newcomer dog, feeling out-numbered, lowered his tail and retired under the wagon with raised hackles and bared teeth.

The man on the wagon seat called out, 'That's a bad dog in a fight when he gets started.'

Elisa laughed. 'I see he is. How soon does he generally get started?'

The man caught up her laughter and echoed it heartily. 'Sometimes not for weeks and weeks,' he said. He climbed stiffly down, over the wheel. The horse and the donkey drooped like unwatered flowers.

Elisa saw that he was a very big man. Although his hair and beard were greying, he did not look old. His worn black suit was wrinkled and spotted with grease. The laughter had disappeared from his face and eyes the moment his laughing voice ceased. His eyes were dark, and they were full of the brooding that gets in the eyes of teamsters and of sailors. The calloused hands he rested on the wire fence were cracked, and every crack was a black line. He took off his battered hat.

'I'm off my general road, ma'am,' he said. 'Does this dirt road cut over across the river to the Los Angeles highway?'

Elisa stood up and shoved the thick scissors in her apron pocket. 'Well, yes, it does, but it winds around and then fords the river. I don't think your team could pull through the sand.'

He replied with some asperity, 'It might surprise you what them beasts can pull through.'

'When they get started?' she asked.

He smiled for a second. 'Yes. When they get started.'

'Well,' said Elisa, 'I think you'll save time if you go back to the Salinas road and pick up the highway there.'

He drew a big finger down the chicken wire and made it sing. 'I ain't in any hurry, ma'am. I go from Seattle to San Diego and back every year. Takes all my time. About six months each way. I aim to follow nice weather.'

Elisa took off her gloves and stuffed them in the apron pocket with the scissors. She touched the under edge of her man's hat, searching for fugitive hairs. 'That sounds like a nice kind of a way to live,' she said.

He leaned confidentially over the fence. 'Maybe you noticed the writing on my wagon. I mend pots and sharpen knives and scissors. You got any of them things to do?'

'Oh, no,' she said quickly. 'Nothing like that.' Her eyes hardened with resistance.

'Scissors is the worst thing,' he explained. 'Most people just ruin scissors trying to sharpen 'em, but I know how. I got a special tool. It's a little bobbit kind of thing, and patented. But it sure does the trick.'

'No. My scissors are all sharp.'

'All right, then. Take a pot,' he continued earnestly, 'a bent pot, or a pot with a hole. I can make it like new so you don't have to buy no new ones. That's a saving for you.'

'No,' she said shortly. 'I tell you I have nothing like that for you to do.'

His face fell to an exaggerated sadness. His voice took on a whining undertone. 'I ain't had a thing to do today. Maybe I won't have no supper tonight. You see I'm off my regular road. I know folks on the highway clear from Seattle to San Diego. They save their things for me to sharpen up because they know I do it so good and save them money.'

'I'm sorry,' Elisa said irritably. 'I haven't anything for you to do.'

His eyes left her face and fell to searching the ground. They roamed about until they came to the chrysanthemum bed where she had been working. 'What's them plants, ma'am?'

The irritation and resistance melted from Elisa's

face. 'Oh, those are chrysanthemums, giant whites and yellows. I raise them every year, bigger than anybody around here.'

'Kind of a long-stemmed flower? Looks like a quick puff of colored smoke?' he asked.

'That's it. What a nice way to describe them.'

'They smell kind of nasty till you get used to them,' he said.

'It's a good bitter smell,' she retorted, 'not nasty at all.'

He changed his tone quickly. 'I like the smell myself.'

'I had ten-inch blooms this year,' she said.

The man leaned farther over the fence. 'Look. I know a lady down the road a piece, has got the nicest garden you ever seen. Got nearly every kind of flower but no chrysantheums. Last time I was mending a copper-bottom washtub for her (that's a hard job but I do it good), she said to me, "If you ever run acrost some nice chrysantheums I wish you'd try to get me a few seeds." That's what she told me.'

Elisa's eyes grew alert and eager. 'She couldn't have known much about chrysanthemums. You *can* raise them from seed, but it's much easier to root the little sprouts you see there.'

'Oh,' he said. 'I s'pose I can't take none to her, then.'

'Why yes you can,' Elisa cried. 'I can put some in damp sand, and you can carry them right along with you. They'll take root in the pot if you keep them damp. And then she can transplant them.'

'She'd sure like to have some, ma'am. You say they're nice ones?'

'Beautiful,' she said. 'Oh, beautiful.' Her eyes shone. She tore off the battered hat and shook out her dark pretty hair. 'I'll put them in a flower pot, and you can take them right with you. Come into the yard.'

While the man came through the picket gate Elisa ran excitedly along the geranium-bordered path to the back of the house. And she returned carrying a big red flower pot. The gloves were forgotten now. She kneeled on the ground by the starting bed and dug up the sandy soil with her fingers and scooped it into the bright new flower pot. Then she picked up the little pile of shoots she had prepared. With her strong fingers she pressed them into the sand and tamped around them with her knuckles. The man stood over her. 'I'll tell you what to do,' she said. 'You remember so you can tell the lady.'

'Yes, I'll try to remember.'

'Well, look. These will take root in about a month. Then she must set them out, about a foot apart in good rich earth like this, see?' She lifted a handful of dark soil for him to look at. 'They'll grow fast and tall. Now remember this: In July tell her to cut them down, about eight inches from the ground.'

'Before they bloom?' he asked.

'Yes, before they bloom.' Her face was tight with eagerness. 'They'll grow right up again. About the last of September the buds will start.'

She stopped and seemed perplexed. 'It's the budding that takes the most care,' she said hesitantly. 'I don't know how to tell you.' She looked deep into his eyes, searchingly. Her mouth opened a little, and she seemed to be listening. 'I'll try to tell you,' she said. 'Did you ever hear of planting hands?'

'Can't say I have, ma'am.'

'Well, I can only tell you what it feels like. It's when you're picking off the buds you don't want. Everything goes right down into your fingertips. You watch your fingers work. They do it themselves. You can feel how it is. They pick and pick the buds. They never make a mistake. They're with the plant. Do you see? Your fingers and the plant. You can feel that, right up your arm. They know. They never make a mistake. You can feel it. When you're like that you can't do anything wrong. Do you see that? Can you understand that?'

She was kneeling on the ground looking up at him. Her breast swelled passionately.

The man's eyes narrowed. He looked away self-consciously. 'Maybe I know,' he said. 'Sometimes in the night in the wagon there –'

Elisa's voice grew husky. She broke in on him, 'I've never lived as you do, but I know what you mean. When the night is dark – why, the stars are sharp-pointed, and there's quiet. Why, you rise up and up! Every pointed star gets driven into your body. It's like that. Hot and sharp and – lovely.'

Kneeling there, her hand went out toward his legs in the greasy black trousers. Her hesitant fingers almost touched the cloth. Then her hand dropped to the ground. She crouched low like a fawning dog.

He said, 'It's nice, just like you say. Only when you don't have no dinner, it ain't.'

She stood up then, very straight, and her face was ashamed. She held the flower pot out to him and placed it gently in his arms. 'Here. Put it in your wagon, on the seat, where you can watch it. Maybe I can find something for you to do.'

At the back of the house she dug in the can pile and found two old and battered aluminum saucepans. She carried them back and gave them to him. 'Here, maybe you can fix these.'

His manner changed. He became professional. 'Good as new I can fix them.' At the back of his wagon he set a little anvil, and out of an oily tool box dug a small machine hammer. Elisa came through the gate to watch him while he pounded out the dents in the kettles. His mouth grew sure and knowing. At a difficult part of the work he sucked his under-lip.

'You sleep right in the wagon?' Elisa asked.

'Right in the wagon, ma'am. Rain or shine I'm dry as a cow in there.'

'It must be nice,' she said. 'It must be very nice. I wish women could do such things.'

'It ain't the right kind of a life for a woman.'

Her upper lip raised a little, showing her teeth. 'How do you know? How can you tell?' she said.

'I don't know, ma'am,' he protested. 'Of course I don't know. Now here's your kettles, done. You don't have to buy no new ones.'

'How much?'

'Oh, fifty cents'll do. I keep my prices down and my work good. That's why I have all them satisfied customers up and down the highway.'

Elisa brought him a fifty-cent piece from the house and dropped it in his hand. 'You might be surprised to have a rival some time. I can sharpen scissors, too. And I can beat the dents out of little pots. I could show you what a woman might do.'

He put his hammer back in the oily box and shoved the little anvil out of sight. 'It would be a lonely life for a woman, ma'am, and a scary life, too, with animals creeping under the wagon all night.' He climbed over the singletree, steadying himself with a hand on the burro's white rump. He settled himself in the seat, picked up the lines. 'Thank you kindly, ma'am,' he said. 'I'll do like you told me; I'll go back and catch the Salinas road.'

'Mind,' she called, 'if you're long in getting there, keep the sand damp.'

'Sand, ma'am? . . . Sand? Oh, sure. You mean around the chrysantheums. Sure I will.' He clucked his tongue. The beasts leaned luxuriously into their collars. The mongrel dog took his place between the back wheels. The wagon turned and crawled out the entrance road and back the way it had come, along the river.

Elisa stood in front of her wire fence watching the slow progress of the caravan. Her shoulders were straight, her head thrown back, her eyes half-closed, so that the scene came vaguely into them. Her lips moved silently, forming the words 'Good-bye – good-bye.' Then she whispered, 'That's a bright direction. There's a glowing there.' The sound of her whisper startled her. She shook herself free and looked about to see whether anyone had been listening. Only the dogs had heard. They lifted their heads toward her from their sleeping in the dust, and then stretched out their chins and settled asleep again. Elisa turned and ran hurriedly into the house.

In the kitchen she reached behind the stove and felt the water tank. It was full of hot water from the noonday cooking. In the bathroom she tore off her soiled clothes and flung them into the corner. And then she scrubbed herself with a little block of pumice, legs and thighs, loins and chest and arms, until her skin was scratched and red. When she had dried herself she stood in front of a mirror in her bedroom and looked at her body. She tightened her stomach and threw out her chest. She turned and looked over her shoulder at her back.

After a while she began to dress, slowly. She put on her newest underclothing and her nicest stockings and the dress which was the symbol of her prettiness. She worked carefully on her hair, penciled her eyebrows and rouged her lips.

Before she was finished she heard the little thunder of hoofs and the shouts of Henry and his helper as they drove the red steers into the corral. She heard the gate bang shut and set herself for Henry's arrival.

His step sounded on the porch. He entered the house calling, 'Elisa, where are you?'

'In my room, dressing. I'm not ready. There's hot water for your bath. Hurry up. It's getting late.'

When she heard him splashing in the tub, Elisa laid his dark suit on the bed, and shirt and socks and tie beside it. She stood his polished shoes on the floor beside the bed. Then she went to the porch and sat primly and stiffly down. She looked toward the river road where the willow-line was still yellow with frosted leaves so that under the high grey fog they seemed a thin band of sunshine. This was the only color in the grey afternoon. She sat unmoving for a long time. Her eyes blinked rarely.

Henry came banging out of the door, shoving his tie inside his vest as he came. Elisa stiffened and her face grew tight. Henry stopped short and looked at her. 'Why – why, Elisa. You look so nice!'

'Nice? You think I look nice? What do you mean by "nice"?'

Henry blundered on. 'I don't know. I mean you look different, strong and happy.'

'I am strong? Yes, strong. What do you mean "strong"?'

He looked bewildered. 'You're playing some kind of a game,' he said helplessly. 'It's a kind of a play. You look strong enough to break a calf over your knee, happy enough to eat it like a water-melon.'

For a second she lost her rigidity. 'Henry! Don't talk like that. You didn't know what you said.' She grew complete again. 'I'm strong,' she boasted. 'I never knew before how strong.'

Henry looked down toward the tractor shed, and when he brought his eyes back to her, they were his own again. 'I'll get out the car. You can put on your coat while I'm starting.'

Elisa went into the house. She heard him drive to the gate and idle down his motor, and then she took a long time to put on her hat. She pulled it here and pressed it there. When Henry turned the motor off she slipped into her coat and went out.

The little roadster bounced along on the dirt road by the river, raising the birds and driving the rabbits into the brush. Two cranes flapped heavily over the willow-line and dropped into the river-bed.

Far ahead on the road Elisa saw a dark speck. She knew.

She tried not to look as they passed it, but her

eyes would not obey. She whispered to herself sadly, 'He might have thrown them off the road. That wouldn't have been much trouble, not very much. But he kept the pot,' she explained. 'He had to keep the pot. That's why he couldn't get them off the road.'

The roadster turned a bend and she saw the caravan ahead. She swung full around toward her husband so she could not see the little covered wagon and the mismatched team as the car passed them.

In a moment it was over. The thing was done. She did not look back.

She said loudly, to be heard above the motor, 'It will be good, tonight, a good dinner.'

'Now you've changed again,' Henry complained. He took one hand from the wheel and patted her knee. 'I ought to take you in to dinner oftener. It would be good for both of us. We get so heavy out on the ranch.'

'Henry,' she asked, 'could we have wine at dinner?'

'Sure we could. Say! That will be fine.'

She was silent for a while; then she said, 'Henry, at those prize fights, do the men hurt each other very much?'

'Sometimes a little, not often. Why?'

'Well, I've read how they break noses, and blood runs down their chests. I've read how the fighting gloves get heavy and soggy with blood.'

He looked around at her. 'What's the matter, Elisa? I didn't know you read things like that.' He brought the car to a stop, then turned to the right over the Salinas River bridge.

'Do any women ever go to the fights?' she asked.

'Oh, sure, some. What's the matter, Elisa? Do you want to go? I don't think you'd like it, but I'll take you if you really want to go.'

She relaxed limply in the seat. 'Oh, no. No. I don't want to go. I'm sure I don't.' Her face was turned away from him. 'It will be enough if we can have wine. It will be plenty.' She turned up her coat collar so he could not see that she was crying weakly – like an old woman.

Breakfast

This thing fills me with pleasure. I don't know why, I can see it in the smallest detail. I find myself recalling it again and again, each time bringing more detail out of sunken memory, remembering brings the curious warm pleasure.

It was very early in the morning. The eastern mountains were black-blue, but behind them the light stood up faintly colored at the mountain rims with a washed red, growing colder, greyer and darker as it went up and overhead until, at a place near the west, it merged with pure night.

And it was cold, not painfully so, but cold enough so that I rubbed my hands and shoved them deep into my pockets, and I hunched my shoulders up and scuffled my feet on the ground. Down in the valley where I was, the earth was that lavender grey of dawn. I walked along a country road and ahead of me I saw a tent that was only a little lighter grey than the ground. Beside the tent there was a flash of orange fire seeping out of the cracks of an old rusty iron stove. Grey smoke spurted up out of the stubby stovepipe, spurted up a long way before it spread out and dissipated.

I saw a young woman beside the stove, really a

girl. She was dressed in a faded cotton skirt and waist. As I came close I saw that she carried a baby in a crooked arm and the baby was nursing, its head under her waist out of the cold. The mother moved about, poking the fire, shifting the rusty lids of the stove to make a greater draft, opening the oven door; and all the time the baby was nursing, but that didn't interfere with the mother's work, nor with the light quick gracefulness of her movements. There was something very precise and practiced in her movements. The orange fire flicked out of the cracks in the stove and threw dancing reflections on the tent.

I was close now and I could smell frying bacon and baking bread, the warmest, pleasantest odors I know. From the east the light grew swiftly. I came near to the stove and stretched my hands out to it and shivered all over when the warmth struck me. Then the tent flap jerked up and a young man came out and an older man followed him. They were dressed in new blue dungarees and in new dungaree coats with brass buttons shining. They were sharp-faced men, and they looked much alike.

The younger had a dark stubble beard and the older had a grey stubble beard. Their heads and faces were wet, their hair dripped with water, and water stood out on their stiff beards and their cheeks shone with water. Together they stood looking quietly at the lightening east; they yawned together and looked at the light on the hill rims. They turned and saw me.

'Morning,' said the older man. His face was neither friendly nor unfriendly.

'Morning, sir,' I said.

'Morning,' said the young man.

The water was slowly drying on their faces. They came to the stove and warmed their hands at it.

The girl kept to her work, her face averted and her eyes on what she was doing. Her hair was tied back out of her eyes with a string and it hung down her back and swayed as she worked. She set tin cups on a big packing box, set tin plates and knives and forks out too. Then she scooped fried bacon out of the deep grease and laid it on a big tin platter, and the bacon cricked and rustled as it grew crisp. She opened the rusty oven door and took out a square pan full of high big biscuits.

When the smell of that hot bread came out, both of the men inhaled deeply. The young man said softly, 'Keerist!'

The elder man turned to me, 'Had you breakfast?'

'No.'

'Well, sit down with us, then.'

That was the signal. We went to the packing case and squatted on the ground about it. The young man asked, 'Picking cotton?'

'No.'

'We have twelve days' work so far,' the young man said.

The girl spoke from the stove. 'They even got new clothes.'

The two men looked down at their new dungarees and they both smiled a little.

The girl set out the platter of bacon, the brown high biscuits, a bowl of bacon gravy and a pot of coffee, and then she squatted down by the box too. The baby was still nursing, its head up under her waist out of the cold. I could hear the sucking noises it made.

We filled our plates, poured bacon gravy over our biscuits and sugared our coffee. The older man filled his mouth full and he chewed and chewed and swallowed. Then he said, 'God Almighty, it's good,' and he filled his mouth again.

The young man said, 'We been eating good for twelve days.'

We all ate quickly, frantically, and refilled our plates and ate quickly again until we were full and warm. The hot bitter coffee scalded our throats. We threw the last little bit with the grounds in it on the earth and refilled our cups.

There was color in the light now, a reddish gleam that made the air seem colder. The two men faced the east and their faces were lighted by the dawn, and I looked up for a moment and saw the image of the mountain and the light coming over it reflected in the older man's eyes.

Then the two men threw the grounds from their cups on the earth and they stood up together. 'Got to get going,' the older man said.

The younger turned to me. "F'you want to pick cotton, we could maybe get you on.'

'No. I got to go along. Thanks for breakfast.'

The older man waved his hand in a negative. 'O.K. Glad to have you.' They walked away together. The air was blazing with light at the eastern skyline. And I walked away down the country road.

That's all. I know, of course, some of the reasons why it was pleasant. But there was some element of great beauty there that makes the rush of warmth when I think of it.

The Vigilante

The great surge of emotion, the milling and shouting of the people fell gradually to silence in the town park. A crowd of people still stood under the elm trees, vaguely lighted by a blue street light two blocks away. A tired quiet settled on the people; some members of the mob began to sneak away into the darkness. The park lawn was cut to pieces by the feet of the crowd.

Mike knew it was all over. He could feel the letdown in himself. He was as heavily weary as though he had gone without sleep for several nights, but it was a dream-like weariness, a grey comfortable weariness. He pulled his cap down over his eyes and moved away, but before leaving the park he turned for one last look.

In the center of the mob someone had lighted a twisted newspaper and was holding it up. Mike could see how the flame curled about the feet of the grey naked body hanging from the elm tree. It seemed curious to him that negroes turn a bluish grey when they are dead. The burning newspaper lighted the heads of the up-looking men, silent men and fixed; they didn't move their eyes from the hanged man.

Mike felt a little irritation at whoever it was who was trying to burn the body. He turned to a man who stood beside him in the near-darkness. 'That don't do no good,' he said.

The man moved away without replying.

The newspaper torch went out, leaving the park almost black by contrast. But immediately another twisted paper was lighted and held up against the feet. Mike moved to another watching man. 'That don't do no good,' he repeated. 'He's dead now. They can't hurt him none.'

The second man grunted but did not look away from the flaming paper. 'It's a good job,' he said. 'This'll save the county a lot of money and no sneaky lawyers getting in.'

'That's what I say,' Mike agreed. 'No sneaky lawyers. But it don't do no good to try to burn him.'

The man continued staring toward the flame. 'Well, it can't do much harm, either.'

Mike filled his eyes with the scene. He felt that he was dull. He wasn't seeing enough of it. Here was a thing he would want to remember later so he could tell about it, but the dull tiredness seemed to cut the sharpness off the picture. His brain told him this was a terrible and important affair, but his eyes and his feelings didn't agree. It was just ordinary. Half an hour before, when he had been howling with the mob and fighting for a chance to help pull on the rope, then his chest had been so full that he had found he was crying. But now everything was dead, everything unreal; the dark mob was made up of stiff lay-figures. In the flame-light the faces were as expressionless as wood. Mike felt the stiffness, the unreality in himself, too. He turned away at last and walked out of the park.

The moment he left the outskirts of the mob a cold loneliness fell upon him. He walked quickly along the street wishing that some other man might be walking beside him. The wide street was deserted, empty, as unreal as the park had been. The two steel lines of the car tracks stretched glimmering away down the street under the elec-troliers, and the dark store windows reflected the midnight globes.

A gentle pain began to make itself felt in Mike's chest. He felt with his fingers; the muscles were sore. Then he remembered. He was in the front line of the mob when it rushed the closed jail door. A driving line forty men deep had crushed Mike against the door like the head of a ram. He had hardly felt it then, and even now the pain seemed to have the dull quality of loneliness.

Two blocks ahead the burning neon word BEER hung over the sidewalk. Mike hurried toward it. He hoped there would be people there, and talk, to remove this silence; and he hoped the men wouldn't have been to the lynching.

The bartender was alone in his little bar, a small, middle-aged man with a melancholy moustache and an expression like an aged mouse, wise and unkempt and fearful.

He nodded quickly as Mike came in. 'You look like you been walking in your sleep,' he said.

Mike regarded him with wonder. 'That's just how I feel, too, like I been walking in my sleep.'

'Well, I can give you a shot if you want.'

Mike hesitated. 'No – I'm kind of thirsty. I'll take a beer. . . . Was you there?'

The little man nodded his mouse-like head again. 'Right at the last, after he was all up and it was all over. I figured a lot of the fellas would be thirsty, so I came back and opened up. Nobody but you so far. Maybe I was wrong.'

'They might be along later,' said Mike. 'There's a lot of them still in the park. They cooled off, though. Some of them trying to burn him with newspapers. That don't do no good.'

'Not a bit of good,' said the little bartender. He twitched his thin moustache.

Mike knocked a few grains of celery salt into his beer and took a long drink. 'That's good,' he said. 'I'm kind of dragged out.'

The bartender leaned close to him over the bar, his eyes were bright. 'Was you there all the time – to the jail and everything?'

Mike drank again and then looked through his beer and watched the beads of bubbles rising from the grains of salt in the bottom of the glass. 'Everything,' he said. 'I was one of the first in the jail, and I helped pull on the rope. There's times when citizens got to take the law in their own hands. Sneaky lawyer comes along and gets some fiend out of it.'

The mousy head jerked up and down. 'You Goddam' right,' he said. 'Lawyers can get them out of anything. I guess the nigger was guilty all right.'

'Oh, sure! Somebody said he even confessed.'

The head came close over the bar again. 'How did it start, mister? I was only there after it was all over, and then I only stayed a minute and then came back to open up in case any of the fellas might want a glass of beer.'

Mike drained his glass and pushed it out to be filled. 'Well, of course everybody knew it was going to happen. I was in a bar across from the jail. Been there all afternoon. A guy came in and says, "What are we waiting for?" So we went across the street, and a lot more guys was there and a lot more come. We all stood there and yelled. Then the sheriff come out and made a speech, but we yelled him down. A guy with a twenty-two rifle went along the street and shot out the street lights. Well, then we rushed the jail doors and bust them. The sheriff wasn't going to do nothing. It wouldn't do him no good to shoot a lot of honest men to save a nigger fiend.'

'And election coming on, too,' the bartender put in.

'Well, the sheriff started yelling, "Get the right

man, boys, for Christ's sake get the right man. He's in the fourth cell down."

'It was kind of pitiful,' Mike said slowly. 'The other prisoners were so scared. We could see them through the bars. I never seen such faces.'

The bartender excitedly poured himself a small glass of whiskey and poured it down. 'Can't blame 'em much. Suppose you was in for thirty days and a lynch mob came through. You'd be scared they'd get the wrong man.'

'That's what I say. It was kind of pitiful. Well, we got to the nigger's cell. He just stood stiff with his eyes closed like he was dead drunk. One of the guys slugged him down and he got up, and then somebody else socked him and he went over and hit his head on the cement floor.' Mike leaned over the bar and tapped the polished wood with his fore-finger. "Course this is only my idea, but I think that killed him. Because I helped get his clothes off, and he never made a wiggle, and when we strung him up he didn't jerk around none. No, sir. I think he was dead all the time, after that second guy smacked him.'

'Well, it's all the same in the end.'

'No, it ain't. You like to do the thing right. He had it coming to him, and he should have got it.' Mike reached into his trousers pocket and brought out a piece of torn blue denim. 'That's a piece of the pants he had on.'

The bartender bent close and inspected the

cloth. He jerked his head up at Mike. 'I'll give you a buck for it.'

'Oh no, you won't!'

'All right. I'll give you two bucks for half of it.'

Mike looked suspiciously at him. 'What you want it for?'

'Here! Give me your glass! Have a beer on me. I'll pin it up on the wall with a little card under it. The fellas that come in will like to look at it.'

Mike haggled the piece of cloth in two with his pocket knife and accepted two silver dollars from the bartender.

'I know a show card writer,' the little man said. 'Comes in every day. He'll print me up a nice little card to go under it.' He looked wary. 'Think the sheriff will arrest anybody?'

''Course not. What's he want to start any trouble for? There was a lot of votes in that crowd tonight. Soon as they all go away, the sheriff will come and cut the nigger down and clean up some.'

The bartender looked toward the door. 'I guess I was wrong about the fellas wanting a drink. It's getting late.'

'I guess I'll get along home. I feel tired.'

'If you go south, I'll close up and walk a ways with you. I live on south Eighth.'

'Why, that's only two blocks from my house. I live on south Sixth. You must go right past my house. Funny I never saw you around.'

The bartender washed Mike's glass and took off

John Steinbeck

the long apron. He put on his hat and coat, walked
to the door and switched off the red neon sign and
the house lights. For a moment the two men stood
on the sidewalk looking back toward the park. The
city was silent. There was no sound from the park.
A policeman walked along a block away, turning
his flash into the store windows.

'You see?' said Mike. 'Just like nothing happened.'

'Well, if the fellas wanted a glass of beer they
must have gone someplace else.'

'That's what I told you,' said Mike.

They swung along the empty street and turned
south, out of the business district. 'My name's
Welch,' the bartender said. 'I only been in this town
about two years.'

The loneliness had fallen on Mike again. 'It's
funny –' he said, and then, 'I was born right in this
town, right in the house I live in now. I got a wife
but no kids. Both of us born right in this town.
Everybody knows us.'

They walked on for a few blocks. The stores
dropped behind and the nice houses with bushy
gardens and cut lawns lined the street. The tall
shade trees were shadowed on the sidewalk by the
street lights. Two night dogs went slowly by,
smelling at each other.

Welch said softly – 'I wonder what kind of a
fella he was – the nigger, I mean.'

Mike answered out of his loneliness. 'The papers

32

all said he was a fiend. I read all the papers. That's
what they all said.'

'Yes, I read them, too. But it makes you wonder
about him. I've known some pretty nice niggers.'

Mike turned his head and spoke protestingly.
'Well, I've knew some dam' fine niggers myself.
I've worked right 'longside some niggers and they
was as nice as any white man you could want to
meet. – But not no fiends.'

His vehemence silenced little Welch for a
moment. Then he said, 'You couldn't tell, I guess,
what kind of a fella he was?'

'No – he just stood there stiff, with his mouth
shut and his eyes tight closed and his hands right
down at his sides. And then one of the guys
smacked him. It's my idea he was dead when we
took him out.'

Welch sidled close on the walk. 'Nice gardens
along here. Must take a lot of money to keep them
up.' He walked even closer, so that his shoulder
touched Mike's arm. 'I never been to a lynching.
How's it make you feel – afterwards?'

Mike shied away from the contact. 'It don't make
you feel nothing.' He put down his head and
increased his pace. The little bartender had nearly
to trot to keep up. The street lights were fewer. It
was darker and safer. Mike burst out, 'Makes you
feel kind of cut off and tired, but kind of satisfied,
too. Like you done a good job – but tired and kind
of sleepy.' He slowed his steps. 'Look, there's a

light in the kitchen. That's where I live. My old lady's waiting up for me.' He stopped in front of his little house.

Welch stood nervously beside him. 'Come into my place when you want a glass of beer – or a shot. Open till midnight. I treat my friends right.' He scampered away like an aged mouse.

Mike called, 'Good night.'

He walked around the side of his house and went in the back door. His thin, petulant wife was sitting by the open gas oven warming herself. She turned complaining eyes on Mike where he stood in the doorway.

Then her eyes widened and hung on his face. 'You been with a woman,' she said hoarsely. 'What woman you been with?'

Mike laughed. 'You think you're pretty slick, don't you? You're a slick one, ain't you? What makes you think I been with a woman?'

She said fiercely, 'You think I can't tell by the look on your face that you been with a woman?'

'All right,' said Mike. 'If you're so slick and know-it-all, I won't tell you nothing. You can just wait for the morning paper.'

He saw doubt come into the dissatisfied eyes. 'Was it the nigger?' she asked. 'Did they get the nigger? Everybody said they was going to.'

'Find out for yourself if you're so slick. I ain't going to tell you nothing.'

He walked through the kitchen and went into

the bathroom. A little mirror hung on the wall. Mike took off his cap and looked at his face. 'By God, she was right,' he thought. 'That's just exactly how I do feel.'

The Murder

This happened a number of years ago in Monterey County, in central California. The Cañon del Castillo is one of those valleys in the Santa Lucia range which lie between its many spurs and ridges. From the main Cañon del Castillo a number of little arroyos cut back into the mountains, oak-wooded canyons, heavily brushed with poison oak and sage. At the head of the canyon there stands a tremendous stone castle, buttressed and towered like those strongholds the Crusaders put up in the path of their conquests. Only a close visit to the castle shows it to be a strange accident of time and water and erosion working on soft, stratified sand-stone. In the distance the ruined battlements, the gates, the towers, even the arrow slits, require little imagination to make out.

Below the castle, on the nearly level floor of the canyon, stand the old ranch house, a weathered and mossy barn and a warped feeding-shed for cattle. The house is deserted; the doors, swinging on rusted hinges, squeal and bang on nights when the wind courses down from the castle. Not many people visit the house. Sometimes a crowd of boys tramp through the rooms, peering into empty closets and loudly defying the ghosts they deny.

Jim Moore, who owns the land, does not like to have people about the house. He rides up from his new house, farther down the valley, and chases the boys away. He has put 'No Trespassing' signs on his fences to keep curious and morbid people out. Sometimes he thinks of burning the old house down, but then a strange and powerful relation with the swinging doors, the blind and desolate windows, forbids the destruction. If he should burn the house he would destroy a great and important piece of his life. He knows that when he goes to town with his plump and still pretty wife, people turn and look at his retreating back with awe and some admiration.

Jim Moore was born in the old house and grew up in it. He knew every grained and weathered board of the barn, every smooth, worn manger-rack. His mother and father were both dead when he was thirty. He celebrated his majority by raising a beard. He sold the pigs and decided never to have any more. At last he bought a fine Guernsey bull to improve his stock, and he began to go to Monterey on Saturday nights, to get drunk and to talk with the noisy girls of the Three Star.

Within a year Jim Moore married Jelka Šepić, a Jugo-Slav girl, daughter of a heavy and patient farmer of Pine Canyon. Jim was not proud of her foreign family, of her many brothers and sisters and cousins, but he delighted in her beauty. Jelka had eyes as large and questioning as a doe's eyes. Her nose was thin and sharply faceted, and her lips werc dccp and soft. Jelka's skin always startled Jim, for between night and night he forgot how beautiful it was. She was so smooth and quiet and gentle, such a good housekeeper, that Jim often thought with disgust of her father's advice on the wedding day. The old man, bleary and bloated with festival beer, elbowed Jim in the ribs and grinned suggestively, so that his little dark eyes almost disappeared behind puffed and wrinkled lids.

'Don't be big fool, now,' he said. 'Jelka is Slav girl. He's not like American girl. If he is bad, beat him. If he's good too long, beat him too. I beat his mama. Papa beat my mama. Slav girl! He's not like a man that don't beat hell out of him.'

'I wouldn't beat Jelka,' Jim said.

The father giggled and nudged him again with his elbow. 'Don't be big fool,' he warned. 'Sometime you see.' He rolled back to the beer barrel.

Jim found soon enough that Jelka was not like American girls. She was very quiet. She never spoke at first, but only answered his questions, and then with soft short replies. She learned her husband as she learned passages of Scripture. After they had been married a while, Jim never wanted for any habitual thing in the house but Jelka had it ready for him before he could ask. She was a fine wife, but there was no companionship in her. She never talked. Her great eyes followed him, and when he smiled, sometimes she smiled too, a distant and covered smile. Her knitting and mending and sewing were interminable. There she sat, watching her wise hands, and she seemed to regard with wonder and pride the little white hands that could do such nice and useful things. She was so much like an animal that sometimes Jim patted her head and neck under the same impulse that made him stroke a horse.

In the house Jelka was remarkable. No matter what time Jim came in from the hot dry range or from the bottom farm land, his dinner was exactly, steamingly ready for him. She watched while he ate, and pushed the dishes close when he needed them, and filled his cup when it was empty.

Early in the marriage he told her things that happened on the farm, but she smiled at him as a foreigner does who wishes to be agreeable even though he doesn't understand.

'The stallion cut himself on the barbed wire,' he said.

And she replied, 'Yes,' with a downward inflection that held neither question nor interest.

He realized before long that he could not get in touch with her in any way. If she had a life apart, it was so remote as to be beyond his reach. The barrier in her eyes was not one that could be removed, for it was neither hostile nor intentional.

At night he stroked her straight black hair and

her unbelievably smooth golden shoulders, and she whimpered a little with pleasure. Only in the climax of embrace did she seem to have a life apart, fierce and passionate. And then immediately she lapsed into the alert and painfully dutiful wife.

'Why don't you ever talk to me?' he demanded. 'Don't you want to talk to me?'

'Yes,' she said. 'What do you want me to say?' She spoke the language of his race out of a mind that was foreign to his race.

When a year had passed, Jim began to crave the company of women, the chattery exchange of small talk, the shrill pleasant insults, the shame-sharpened vulgarity. He began to go again to town, to drink and play with the noisy girls of the Three Star. They liked him there for his firm, controlled face and for his readiness to laugh.

'Where's your wife?' they demanded.

'Home in the barn,' he responded. It was a never-failing joke.

Saturday afternoons he saddled a horse and put a rifle in the scabbard in case he should see a deer. Always he asked, 'You don't mind staying alone?'

'No. I don't mind.'

At once he asked, 'Suppose someone should come?'

Her eyes sharpened for a moment, and then she smiled. 'I would send them away,' she said.

'I'll be back about noon tomorrow. It's too far to ride in the night.' He felt that she knew where he was going, but she never protested nor gave any sign of disapproval. 'You should have a baby,' he said.

Her face lighted up. 'Some time God will be good,' she said eagerly.

He was sorry for her loneliness. If only she visited with the other women of the canyon she would be less lonely, but she had no gift for visiting. Once every month or so she put horses to the buckboard and went to spend an afternoon with her mother, and with the brood of brothers and sisters and cousins who lived in her father's house.

'A fine time you'll have,' Jim said to her. 'You'll gabble your crazy language like ducks for a whole afternoon. You'll giggle with that big grown cousin of yours with the embarrassed face. If I could find any fault with you, I'd call you a damn foreigner.' He remembered how she blessed the bread with the sign of the cross before she put it in the oven, how she knelt at the bedside every night, how she had a holy picture tacked to the wall in the closet.

One Saturday of a hot dusty June, Jim cut oats in the farm flat. The day was long. It was after six o'clock when the mower tumbled the last band of oats. He drove the clanking machine up into the barnyard and backed it into the implement shed, and there he unhitched the horses and turned them out to graze on the hills over Sunday. When he entered the kitchen Jelka was just putting his

dinner on the table. He washed his hands and face
and sat down to eat.

'I'm tired,' he said, 'but I think I'll go to
Monterey anyway. There'll be a full moon.'

Her soft eyes smiled.

'I'll tell you what I'll do,' he said. 'If you would
like to go, I'll hitch up a rig and take you with me.'

She smiled again and shook her head. 'No, the
stores would be closed. I would rather stay here.'

'Well, all right, I'll saddle a horse then. I didn't
think I was going. The stock's all turned out.
Maybe I can catch a horse easy. Sure you don't
want to go?'

'If it was early, and I could go to the stores –
but it will be ten o'clock when you get there.'

'Oh, no – well, anyway, on horseback I'll make
it a little after nine.'

Her mouth smiled to itself, but her eyes watched
him for the development of a wish. Perhaps
because he was tired from the long day's work, he
demanded, 'What are you thinking about?'

'Thinking about? I remember, you used to ask
that nearly every day when we were first married.'

'But what are you?' he insisted irritably.

'Oh – I'm thinking about the eggs under the
black hen.' She got up and went to the big calendar
on the wall. 'They will hatch tomorrow or maybe
Monday.'

It was almost dusk when he had finished shaving
and putting on his blue serge suit and his new

boots. Jelka had the dishes washed and put away. As Jim went through the kitchen he saw that she had taken the lamp to the table near the window, and that she sat beside it knitting a brown wool sock.

'Why do you sit there tonight?' he asked. 'You always sit over here. You do funny things sometimes.'

Her eyes arose slowly from her flying hands. 'The moon,' she said quietly. 'You said it would be full tonight. I want to see the moon rise.'

'But you're silly. You can't see it from that window. I thought you knew direction better than that.'

She smiled remotely. 'I will look out of the bedroom window, then.'

Jim put on his black hat and went out. Walking through the dark empty barn, he took a halter from the rack. On the grassy sidehill he whistled high and shrill. The horses stopped feeding and moved slowly in toward him, and stopped twenty feet away. Carefully he approached his bay gelding and moved his hand from its rump along its side and up over its neck. The halter-strap clicked in its buckle. Jim turned and led the horse back to the barn. He threw his saddle on and cinched it tight, put his silver-bound bridle over the stiff ears, buckled the throat latch, knotted the tie-rope about the gelding's neck and fastened the neat coil-end to the saddle string. Then he slipped the halter and led the horse to the house. A radiant crown of soft red light lay over the eastern hills. The full moon would rise before the valley had completely lost daylight.

In the kitchen Jelka still knitted by the window. Jim strode to the corner of the room and took up his 30-30 carbine. As he rammed cartridges into the magazine, he said, 'The moon glow is on the hills. If you are going to see it rise, you better go outside now. It's going to be a good red one at rising.'

'In a moment,' she replied, 'when I come to the end here.' He went to her and patted her sleek head.

'Good night. I'll probably be back by noon tomorrow.' Her dusky black eyes followed him out of the door.

Jim thrust the rifle into his saddle-scabbard, and mounted and swung his horse down the canyon. On his right, from behind the blackening hills, the great red moon slid rapidly up. The double light of the day's last afterglow and the rising moon thickened the outlines of the trees and gave a mysterious new perspective to the hills. The dusty oaks shimmered and glowed, and the shade under them was black as velvet. A huge, long-legged shadow of a horse and half a man rode to the left and slightly ahead of Jim. From the ranches near and distant came the sound of dogs tuning up for a night of song. And the roosters crowed, thinking a new dawn had come too quickly. Jim lifted the gelding to a trot. The spattering hoof-steps echoed back from the castle behind him. He thought of blond May at the Three Star in Monterey. 'I'll be late. Maybe someone else'll have her,' he thought. The moon was clear of the hills now.

Jim had gone a mile when he heard the hoof-beats of a horse coming toward him. A horseman cantered up and pulled to a stop. 'That you, Jim?'

'Yes. Oh, hello, George.'

'I was just riding up to your place. I want to tell you – you know the springhead at the upper end of my land?'

'Yes. I know.'

'Well, I was up there this afternoon. I found a dead campfire and a calf's head and feet. The skin was in the fire, half burned, but I pulled it out and it had your brand.'

'The hell,' said Jim. 'How old was the fire?'

'The ground was still warm in the ashes. Last night, I guess. Look, Jim, I can't go up with you. I've got to go to town, but I thought I'd tell you, so you could take a look around.'

Jim asked quietly, 'Any idea how many men?'

'No. I didn't look close.'

'Well, I guess I better go up and look. I was going to town too. But if there are thieves working, I don't want to lose any more stock. I'll cut up through your land if you don't mind, George.'

'I'd go with you, but I've got to go to town. You got a gun with you?'

'Oh yes, sure. Here under my leg. Thanks for telling me.'

'That's all right. Cut through any place you want. Good night.' The neighbor turned his horse and cantered back in the direction from which he had come.

For a few moments Jim sat in the moonlight, looking down at his stilted shadow. He pulled his rifle from its scabbard, levered a cartridge into the chamber, and held the gun across the pommel of his saddle. He turned left from the road, went up the little ridge, through the oak grove, over the grassy hogback and down the other side into the next canyon.

In half an hour he had found the deserted camp. He turned over the heavy, leathery calf's head and felt its dusty tongue to judge by the dryness how long it had been dead. He lighted a match and looked at his brand on the half-burned hide. At last he mounted his horse again, rode over the bald grassy hills and crossed into his own land.

A warm summer wind was blowing on the hilltops. The moon, as it quartered up the sky, lost its redness and turned the color of strong tea. Among the hills the coyotes were singing, and the dogs at the ranch houses below joined them with broken-hearted howling. The dark green oaks below and the yellow summer grass showed their colors in the moonlight.

Jim followed the sound of the cowbells to his

herd, and found them eating quietly, and a few deer feeding with them. He listened long for the sound of hoofbeats or the voices of men on the wind.

It was after eleven when he turned his horse toward home. He rounded the west tower of the sandstone castle, rode through the shadow and out into the moonlight again. Below, the roofs of his barn and house shone dully. The bedroom window cast back a streak of reflection.

The feeding horses lifted their heads as Jim came down through the pasture. Their eyes glinted redly when they turned their heads.

Jim had almost reached the corral fence – he heard a horse stamping in the barn. His hand jerked the gelding down. He listened. It came again, the stamping from the barn. Jim lifted his rifle and dismounted silently. He turned his horse loose and crept toward the barn.

In the blackness he could hear the grinding of the horse's teeth as it chewed hay. He moved along the barn until he came to the occupied stall. After a moment of listening he scratched a match on the butt of his rifle. A saddled and bridled horse was tied in the stall. The bit was slipped under the chin and the cinch loosened. The horse stopped eating and turned its head toward the light.

Jim blew out the match and walked quickly out of the barn. He sat on the edge of the horse trough and looked into the water. His thoughts came so slowly that he put them into words and said them under his breath.

'Shall I look through the window? No. My head would throw a shadow in the room.'

He regarded the rifle in his hand. Where it had been rubbed and handled, the black gun finish had worn off, leaving the metal silvery.

At last he stood up with decision and moved toward the house. At the steps, an extended foot tried each board tenderly before putting his weight on it. The three ranch dogs came out from under the house and shook themselves, stretched and sniffed, wagged their tails and went back to bed.

The kitchen was dark, but Jim knew where every piece of furniture was. He put out his hand and touched the corner of the table, a chair back, the towel hanger, as he went along. He crossed the room so silently that even he could hear only his breath and the whisper of his trouser legs together, and the beating of his watch in his pocket. The bedroom door stood open and spilled a patch of moonlight on the kitchen floor. Jim reached the door at last and peered through.

The moonlight lay on the white bed. Jim saw Jelka lying on her back, one soft bare arm flung across her forehead and eyes. He could not see who the man was, for his head was turned away. Jim watched, holding his breath. Then Jelka twitched in her sleep and the man rolled his head and sighed – Jelka's cousin, her grown, embarrassed cousin.

Jim turned and quickly stole back across the kitchen and down the back steps. He walked up the yard to the water-trough again, and sat down on the edge of it. The moon was white as chalk, and it swam in the water, and lighted the straws and barley dropped by the horses' mouths. Jim could see the mosquito wigglers, tumbling up and down, end over end, in the water, and he could see a newt lying in the sun moss in the bottom of the trough.

He cried a few dry, hard, smothered sobs, and wondered why, for his thought was of the grassed hilltops and of the lonely summer wind whisking along.

His thought turned to the way his mother used to hold a bucket to catch the throat blood when his father killed a pig. She stood as far away as possible and held the bucket at arms'-length to keep her clothes from getting spattered.

Jim dipped his hand into the trough and stirred the moon to broken, swirling streams of light. He wetted his forehead with his damp hands and stood up. This time he did not move so quietly, but he crossed the kitchen on tiptoe and stood in the bedroom door. Jelka moved her arm and opened her eyes a little. Then the eyes sprang wide, then they glistened with moisture. Jim looked into her eyes; his face was empty of expression. A little drop ran out of Jelka's nose and lodged in the hollow of her upper lip. She stared back at him.

Jim cocked the rifle. The steel click sounded through the house. The man on the bed stirred uneasily in his sleep. Jim's hands were quivering. He raised the gun to his shoulder and held it tightly to keep from shaking. Over the sights he saw the little white square between the man's brows and hair. The front sight wavered a moment and then came to rest.

The gun crash tore the air. Jim, still looking down the barrel, saw the whole bed jolt under the blow. A small, black, bloodless hole was in the man's forehead. But behind, the hollow-point bullet took brain and bone and splashed them on the pillow.

Jelka's cousin gurgled in his throat. His hands came crawling out from under the covers like big white spiders, and they walked for a moment, then shuddered and fell quiet.

Jim looked slowly back at Jelka. Her nose was running. Her eyes had moved from him to the end of the rifle. She whined softly, like a cold puppy.

Jim turned in panic. His boot heels beat on the kitchen floor, but outside, he moved slowly toward the water-trough again. There was the taste of salt in his throat, and his heart heaved painfully. He pulled his hat off and dipped his head into the water. Then he leaned over and vomited on the ground. In the house he could hear Jelka moving about. She whimpered like a puppy. Jim straightened up, weak and dizzy.

He walked tiredly through the corral and into the pasture. His saddled horse came at his whistle. Automatically he tightened the cinch, mounted and rode away, down the road to the valley. The squat black shadow traveled under him. The moon sailed high and white. The uneasy dogs barked monotonously.

At daybreak a buckboard and pair trotted up to the ranch yard, scattering the chickens. A deputy sheriff and a coroner sat in the seat. Jim Moore half reclined against his saddle in the wagon-box. His tired gelding followed behind. The deputy sheriff set the brake and wrapped the lines around it. The men dismounted.

Jim asked, 'Do I have to go in? I'm too tired and wrought up to see it now.'

The coroner pulled his lip and studied. 'Oh, I guess not. We'll tend to things and look around.'

Jim sauntered away toward the water-trough. 'Say,' he called, 'kind of clean up a little, will you? You know.'

The men went into the house.

In a few minutes they emerged, carrying the stiffened body between them. It was wrapped up in a comforter. They eased it up into the wagon-box. Jim walked back toward them. 'Do I have to go with you now?'

'Where's your wife, Mr Moore?' the deputy sheriff demanded.

'I don't know,' he said wearily. 'She's somewhere around.'

'You're sure you didn't kill her too?'

'No. I didn't touch her. I'll find her and bring her in this afternoon. That is, if you don't want me to go in with you now.'

'We've got your statement,' the coroner said. 'And by God, we've got eyes, haven't we, Will? Of course there's a technical charge of murder against you, but it'll be dismissed. Always is in this part of the country. Go kind of light on your wife, Mr Moore.'

'I won't hurt her,' said Jim.

He stood and watched the buckboard jolt away. He kicked his feet reluctantly in the dust. The hot June sun showed its face over the hills and flashed viciously on the bedroom window.

Jim went slowly into the house, and brought out a nine-foot, loaded bull whip. He crossed the yard and walked into the barn. And as he climbed the ladder to the hayloft, he heard the high, puppy whimpering start.

When Jim came out of the barn again, he carried Jelka over his shoulder. By the water-trough he set her tenderly on the ground. Her hair was littered with bits of hay. The back of her shirtwaist was streaked with blood.

Jim wetted his bandana at the pipe and washed her bitten lips, and washed her face and brushed back her hair. Her dusky black eyes followed every move he made.

'You hurt me,' she said. 'You hurt me bad.'

He nodded gravely. 'Bad as I could without killing you.'

The sun shone hotly on the ground. A few blowflies buzzed about, looking for the blood.

Jelka's thickened lips tried to smile. 'Did you have any breakfast at all?'

'No,' he said. 'None at all.'

'Well, then, I'll fry you up some eggs.' She struggled painfully to her feet.

'Let me help you,' he said. 'I'll help you get your shirtwaist off. It's drying stuck to your back. It'll hurt.'

'No. I'll do it myself.' Her voice had a peculiar resonance in it. Her dark eyes dwelt warmly on him for a moment, and then she turned and limped into the house.

Jim waited, sitting on the edge of the water-trough. He saw the smoke start out of the chimney and sail straight up into the air. In a very few moments Jelka called him from the kitchen door.

'Come, Jim. Your breakfast.'

Four fried eggs and four thick slices of bacon lay on a warmed plate for him. 'The coffee will be ready in a minute,' she said.

'Won't you eat?'

'No. Not now. My mouth's too sore.'

He ate his eggs hungrily and then looked up at her. Her black hair was combed smooth. She had on a fresh, white shirtwaist. 'We're going to town this afternoon,' he said. 'I'm going to order lumber. We'll build a new house farther down the canyon.'

Her eyes darted to the closed bedroom door and then back to him. 'Yes,' she said. 'That will be good.' And then, after a moment, 'Will you whip me any more – for this?'

'No, not any more, for this.'

Her eyes smiled. She sat down on a chair beside him, and Jim put out his hand and stroked her hair and the back of her neck.

POCKET PENGUINS